I0456654

Eye for an Eye
and other
Short stories

Earl Baron Lacour, Jr.

Nicobar Press

Copyright © 2019 Laurie L. Bolanos

All rights reserved. No part of this publication may be reproduced, distributed or transmitted in any form or by any means, without prior written permission.

Earl Baron Lacour, Jr./Nicobar Press

Publisher's Note: This is a work of fiction. Names, characters, places, and incidents are a product of the author's imagination. Locales and public names are sometimes used for atmospheric purposes. Any resemblance to actual people, living or dead, or to businesses, companies, events, institutions, or locales is completely coincidental.

Book Layout © 2017 BookDesignTemplates.com

Eye for an Eye and other Short Stories/ Earl Baron Lacour, Jr. -- 1st ed.
ISBN **978-1-938125-51-5**

To My Very Own Trudy Ann

Contents

CHAPTER ONE

Eye for an Eye

T he culvert was a little more than four feet in di-
ameter and Adolf was bent nearly double as he
attempted to transverse the distance necessary
to reach the safe house over a mile away. His progress
was agonizingly prolonged by the awkward position
and even with hip boots, the foul fluid at the bottom
saturated his clothes and the exposed parts of his body.
The Kaiser had built the massive sewer system under
Berlin before World War I and Hitler thought it ironic
that the leader of the regime that superseded that government was now practically crawling through it. He
took some measure of satisfaction however, in telling

himself that Stalin, Churchill, and that new man, Truman, would not be capable of such a feat. As he painstakingly inched along, he diverted his attention to the recent circumstances which had catapulted him into his present situation.

The July 1944 bombing attempt on his life had convinced Adolph to change his modus operandi. While in the hospital to remove the almost two hundred wooden splinters from his legs, he ordered the SS to conduct a search for a person who could function as his double. Several men were found and he chose the most p romising individual, a corporal in the German army. The man was surprisingly similar to Hitler in looks and build but Adolph wanted the ruse to be perfect. Feigning fear of further assignation plots, Adolph went into seclusion and used that time for both he and his double to go under the knife. Hitler arranged for plastic surgery for both of them at a prominent Berlin hospital with excellent plastic surgeons on staff. The results were spectacular. The corporal, after growing the trademark moustache, was a dead ringer for the Fuhrer, and Adolph himself had his nose broadened, his chin modified, and had shaved all of his facial hair. Leaving no stone unturned, Hitler had a copy of his dental records sent to the hospital as well and the dental surgeon there duplicated Adolph's dental profile in the corporal's mouth. However, when they left the hospital with Adolph functioning as the imposter's new aide, Hitler knew there were loose ends that needed wrapping up. First, under the guise of protecting himself from further attempts on his life, he replaced all those close to him with new personnel, lest someone would find inconsistencies in the mannerisms of the new Fuhrer. Second, he arrested the corporal's entire family and threatened their well-being to insure his double's complete cooperation. Third, he had the hospital rigged with explosives and detonated them during the next Allied daytime bombing raid thus eliminating the people with knowledge of the identity change. Also, the man impersonating Adolph was several years older and had developed a slight tremor in his hands so Hitler had his medical records altered to indicate a diagnosis of Parkinson's disease. In order to avoid public exposure, Adolph decided to occupy his Berlin bunker and he and the fake Fuhrer arrived there in early 1945.

The location was ideal. He could send orders out by written communique or by telephone and the invention of the magnetic tape recorder permitted speeches over the radio. Also, there was a trap door known only to Adolph that accessed the main sewer line of the city should immediate evacuation become a necessity. However, a problem did arise when Eva Braun, his mistress, insisted on coming to the bunker When she arrived, Adolph, knowing she would detect the deception, took her into his confidence, explaining that it would be to their advantage if a sudden escape was indicated. She agreed to play along with the duplicity and no one in the bunker was the wiser.

As the war pushed into April, it was obvious that the downfall of the Third Reich was eminent. Goebbels and his family moved into the bunker to delay capture and were preparing their own "final solution." The others, Himmler, Goering, etc. were either trying to arrange peace talks with Allies or making personal efforts to extricate themselves from Germany. With both Soviets and the Allies encroaching on Berlin, Adolph decided to put his final plan into action. He contacted a German safe house strategically located along the Berlin sewer with trap door access and told them to prepare to shelter a VIP temporarily until he could be smuggled into Switzerland. He then spoke with Eva Braun outlining this scenario. She and the double would marry, cementing once and for all that the imposter was the Fuhrer. Then, a short time later, Adolph would arrange the fake Hitler's suicide, blaming that act on despondency over the war. Then they would escape through the sewer. His conversation with the double was somewhat different. Hitler said the marriage with Eva was to reassure her and after the event, since she was the only one capable of discerning the real Hitler, she would be eliminated, followed by their escape through the sewer. The plan was put into action. After the wedding ceremony, Adolph announced that the coupe wished to be alone in the bedroom and ordered everyone to evacuate that part of the bunker. Then the three of them went into the room whereupon Hitler and the double forced Eva to swallow a cyanide capsule. While the double was putting Eva's body on the couch, Adolph reached into a drawer, grabbed his Waltham pistol and shot the double point-blank in the right temple. Positioning both bodies on the couch with the gun on the floor by the double's right hand, he hastily wrote a note saying that he and Eva were going to take their own lives and in order to avoid the "Mussolini experience," wished their bodies to be burned. Actually, Adolph didn't care whether the bodies were strung up or not, but he had to make sure that the double's fingerprints were obliterated. Rushing into the other part of the bunker, he confronted the people there, told them he heard a shot, entered the room, saw the bodies, and found the note. In compliance with the written request, he ordered the bodies wrapped in a blanket, then taken outside and burned beyond recognition. While these orders were being carried out, he snuck away, found the trap door, and lowered himself into the sewer where after eighty minutes of tortuous and labored effort, he found himself staring up at the trap door below the safe house.

***

Albert Grunn had been notified to expect important company. He had single handedly operated this home for over a year for patriots of the German cause. Actually, in its hey-day, the home had been a central warehouse featuring a loading bay and fork lift access to the basement, first and second floors. Munitions were stored there and it also served as a repository for the valuables taken from the Holocaust victims as well as the chemical used in their extermination. Now with the war ebbing and the concentration camps overrun, the ammunition had been used up and the "treasure room" for the valuables, still well-fortified with combination locks had been converted into an elaborate bathroom with toilet and shower facilities. However, there were still airtight bags of the dreaded Zyklon B in storage along with clothing and food rations.

Albert cringed when he was reminded of the deadly chemical. He was originally born Jacob Rosenburg to parents of Jewish extraction. His parents, German Jews, had accurately foreseen the political future for their race and thus, by exhausting their life savings, had managed to provide Jacob with a new name and papers attesting to Aryan ancestry. Armed with these false documents, he was able to join the Nazi party and served in various unremarkable positions until being assigned responsibility for the safe house in early 1944. His parents, meanwhile, had been rounded up with the other Jews and sent to a concentration camp. There they were herded into imitation showering facilities where they were subjected to Zyklon B gas and suffered a hideous death. Henceforth, Jacob had prayed for a chance to avenge his parents, but the opportunity had never presented itself.

Jarred back to reality by loud rapping on the trap door, he realized his visitor had arrived. Opening the aperture, he saw a dirty, smelly infuriated man climb out.

"Get me clean clothes and show me the bathing facilities," he ordered. "I wish to wash myself."

Jacob stood speechless and paralyzed by the sight.

"Move," the man shouted. "I am Adolph Hitler in disguise."

***

Adolph had no compunction about revealing his true identity. After all he would have the man terminated once he had left the area.

Jacob ran to the remodeled bathroom, opened the lock, and ushered Adolph inside. Then he retrieved the necessary items from storage. Hitler was already stripping in anticipation of the jets of cleansing water. Jacob deposited the clean clothes next to Hitler, retreated, and locked the now closed doors. As the open bag of Zyklon B hidden in the clothes reacted with the air, Jacob heard screaming and pounding on the door.

"Enjoy your shower Mein Fuhrer," Jacob shouted. "You deserve it!"

CHAPTER TWO

Best Laid Plans

On a beautiful spring morning in the year 2061, Robert Ingram kissed his domestic partner, Marie, goodbye, hopped on a monorail, and started the twenty-minute journey to his assigned place of employment. Air taxi would have been faster, but Robert enjoyed the longer ride, wearing his Wi-Fi goggles to catch up on the news of the day.

Arriving at his workplace, Robert surveyed the 300,000 square foot building and casually walked into his office. He was the manager of the Federal Pharmaceutical Manufacturing Concern located in Phoenix, a state-of-the-art facility containing 20,000 robots supervised by a Quantum Hadron supercomputer named Ezekiel. He rarely encountered human beings at his job, so it was quite surprising that upon entering his supposedly locked office, he came face to face with a dour man in an expensive black suit.

"James Halliway," the man said as he handed James a business card. "Domestic Threat clinician of the division of the Office of Homeland Security. I'm commandeering your plant for the next twelve hours."

Robert was stunned.

After checking the man's credentials, Robert collapsed into his desk chair and blurted, "Why do you need my plant?"

Halliway replied, "There are one-half billion people in the United States today. Our greatest threat is not from terrorist or plague, but over-population. Do you realize that with the demands of Social Security, Medicare, welfare, and unemployment, the U.S. is virtually bankrupt? We can't even afford a military to protect and serve. Something must be done!"

"How can my plant correct this?" Robert interjected.

"Very simply," Halliway responded. "We at D.T.D. have produced a formula which acts like a vaccine. It lasts ten years inside the body, has no side effects, and its action is entirely undetectable to the woman. As soon as an egg is fertilized and implants itself in the womb, chemicals in the formula persuade the body to reabsorb the tissue. Voila! No baby!"

"We already have the necessary ingredients supplied to your robots. We need you now to read this set of instructions to Ezekiel over your voice print so that the production of capsules can begin. Forty million should suffice, the estimated amount for women of reproductive age in our target period, easily achievable in twelve hours with this plant."

Robert jumped up from his chair, screaming. "I can't allow this. This is abortion! The Infant Life Protection Act of 2037 specifically outlaw's abortion in any form, and it has never been repealed."

Holloway replied, "The D.T.D. has taken this into consideration. We have made some inroads in time dilation technology and while we have not been able to send living organisms into the past, we have been successful with inanimate objects. We will thus send these capsules back to 1945, causing a large reduction in the baby boomer generation and a corresponding collateral reduction in our present. U.S. population. The law, enacted almost 100 years in the future, will not be violated."

"Here's the flaw in your plan, "Robert retorted. "The women of 1945 will not just pop these pills in their mouths."

"Oh, yes they will if they are given a reason, "said Holloway. "In 1945, at the end of WWII, people will believe anything that the government tells them. We are prepared to send back proof, that the Japanese, as a part of their war effort introduced drugs into the U.S. water supply that would prevent conception. Roosevelt, then president, died April 12, 1945 and subsequently Truman took over. We will also send back an executive order signed by Roosevelt that in light of the Japanese action, he was requiring all U.S. women of reproductive age to take a government-supplied pill to counter the effect of the Japanese drugs. We will date this the day Roosevelt died, and with an authentic signature on the order, Truman will not oppose it. In fact, Truman will think he was out of the loop, just like he was kept ignorant of the Manhattan project. Enough talk, though. Let's get this project to completion."

Without warning, Holloway pulled a syringe from his pocket and injected something into Robert's arm. "This will make you docile and forgetful," he said. Holloway then gave the written instructions to Robert who read them to Ezekiel.

The orders were transmitted to the robots and the manufacturing of the capsules began. Eight hours later, the operation was completed, the capsules and associated paperwork were ready to be sent back to April, 12, 1945 and Robert, oblivious to everything that occurred, went home.

The next morning of the year 2061, Robert Ingram kissed his wife Genevieve goodbye and jumped into his automobile to start a forty-five-minute drive to the outskirts of Philadelphia where he held the position of Chief X-ray tech at Paul Wagner hospital.

The U.S. population at that moment was approximately 300 million souls, but this was irrelevant information and Robert was not aware of it. He did not miss the technological innovations primarily because the people that would have developed them had never lived. The Domestic Threat Division of the office of Homeland Security had also not been established. However, that was no problem for James Holloway for as it turns out, one of the first people affected by his brain-child pill was a girl who, had she survived, was destined to be his maternal grandmother.

CHAPTER THREE

God is Green

The .38 caliber slug entered into the bone covering the right temporal lobe of Mike Tanny's skull at an angle of twenty degrees. When it penetrated, the ensuing shock wave compressed and disrupted the higher centers of his brain, causing the first of several insults to the sensitive cerebellar tissue. As with all mammalian primates at the point of death, time dilation effects became manifest and while the bullet continued its path through his cortex, the firing dendrites and their synapses poured forth an inventory of memories on a first-in first-out basis for his final perusal.

Surprisingly, there was no pain associated with the bullets passage, and he enjoyed his first remembered sensation—a tactile feeling of being immersed in and surrounded by water. Pleasant though this experience was, he could not savor it as a myriad of other episodes flooded his consciousness. So many, in fact, he could not fully relive them all.

A flashback of his first day of school intrigued him. There he was shivering with dread, not fully understanding the monumental impact this new routine would impose on his future activities. His mother tried to allay his fears.

"You'll make new friends. You'll do fun things. You'll like it."

That day he learned not to trust his parents, and it was with ironic satisfaction that he recalled using the same comments to soothe his mother's trepidation when he enrolled her in the Divine Faith Nursing Home forty years later, almost to the day.

His father, a traveling manufacturer's rep, was a sports freak. After dad had realized his son exhibited no talent for or interest in sports and sporting events, he was, for all intents and purposes a non-entity in Mike's life. The estrangement remained as Mike grew up and when the man prematurely passed as a result of a massive heart attack, Mike felt no great loss.

His high school years were largely unremarkable. He certainly harbored no aspirations of attending college, but due to a modicum of mathematical ability, he was able to secure an account clerk position with a shipping firm upon graduation. The job offered relatively low pay, but required little original thought.

Over the years he progressed upward to assistant bookkeeper, but the real breakthrough, in his estimation, came when he inadvertently slipped on a freshly mopped floor. Although the injury was not that serious, Mike was able to parlay this fall into a permanent disability with an accompanying check along with medical coverage for the rest of his life.

Perpetual security is always a justifiable trade-off for the inconvenience of a limp, he decided.

Mike's relationship with girls/women was initiated in his later teenage years, but after a few dates and futile groping, he came to some life-changing conclusions. First, his libido was almost non-existent. Second, dealing with the opposite sex was more trouble than it was worth.

His thought experiments on the subject were worthy of Einstein. He was able to picture the protracted dating, engagement, wedding, moving from his parent's house into a mortgaged abode (This particular action seemed the most ludicrous to him since he had no siblings and would inherit the familial home outright) and the inevitable children. His extensive analysis of this situation led Mike to accept only platonic female relationships, and those were only when necessary.

When the nursing home called with the news of his mother's death by stroke, Mike became a homeowner.

He celebrated by cleaning out his mother's closets, supplying Good Will with a plethora of old clothes. Almost nothing of his father's remained in the house, but he did locate a trunk in the attic that contained sports memorabilia along with his father's old pistol that was used for target shooting. Mike thought the memorabilia could prove to be valuable, so he left it in the attic. He decided, however, to take his father's hand gun downstairs for protection.

Mike lived contentedly for the next several years. His health had never been much of a concern for him—an ache here, a pain there, a little arthritis in his bad leg—nothing inconsistent with advancing middle age. That changed one night when he woke with excruciating pain, mimicking an electric shock, passing down his left side.

Mike's relationship with the medical profession closely paralleled his relationship with women. However, since doctors were the only legal source of most pain medications, he reluctantly set up an appointment with a local M.D. The diagnosis came back three weeks later.

Advanced non-operable prostate cancer with metastasis to the bone.

Mike was in shock. Being in such a confused state, he only half-comprehended what the doctor was saying.

...terminal, six-month prognosis, hospice, nursing visits, morphine drips, palliative care...

It didn't make sense.

Over the next several days, he resolutely decided that he was not going to put up with strangers in his house and the amount of pain he would have to endure.

As the bullet continued its trajectory through the left side of Mike's skull and deposited itself in a nearby wall, his body slumped back in the chair and his father's pistol slid from his lifeless fingers, clattering on the floor. Of course, philosophers would debate whether the clatter constituted a sound as there was no one to hear it.

The essence that had been Mike Tanny had already exited his body and was being propelled down a long dark tunnel towards a beautiful white light. As it flew down the tunnel, the essence sensed, rather than heard, a voice saying,

"Unplanned termination—insufficient karmic development—recycle."

Instantaneously, the essence experienced a very pleasant and vaguely familiar sensation—that of being immersed in and surrounded by water.

CHAPTER FOUR

The Breakthrough

It was cold in the lab.

It's always cold in the lab, thought Jonas to himself as he checked the petri dishes for signs of progress. He knew that maintaining a regulated environment was critical for accurate experimental data, but he also knew that working in a facility located in Canada, close to the Arctic circle, did not project any added feeling of warmth.

Jonas still literally pinched himself at times to verify that the events leading to his coming here were not a figment of an overactive imagination. Eight months ago, he was completing his PhD in cell biology at Cal Tech. His thesis on cell necrosis had caused somewhat of a stir and he had been awarded a grant by the

National Science Foundation to do post-doctoral work in the field of human life extension. However, a subsequent offer was received which he considered too good to ignore.

Jonas was approached by a man of Middle Eastern extraction known only as "Mo", who purportedly represented a wealthy Arabian Oil sheik. This middle age billionaire had decided that he was not content with the normal human lifespan and was willing to bankroll anyone who could increase it in time for him to benefit. Jonas was inclined to refuse this sort of invitation but when the prospect of unlimited funding and the reality of his own Swiss numbered bank account containing $250, 000 was explained to him, he accepted readily without misgivings.

An old Canadian weather station was subsequently purchased and refitted as a state-of-the-art biological research laboratory. Mo told Jonas the site chosen was isolated in order to minimize distractions since his anonymous benefactor wanted results immediately, if not sooner. Room and board would be provided at the facility and, Mo, along with another man, Al, would act as his assistants.

All work was to be carried on with utmost secrecy and, although computers could be used for controlling data, no access to the internet would be permitted. Jonas' salary would be $150, 000 per month with a lump sum payment of $2,000,000 upon achievement of results that were both independently verifiable and acceptable to the Sheik. The ownership of any successful processes would remain with Jonas, but there would be a moratorium of one year before steps to patent and publish then could be allowed. No one could know of his whereabouts until the project was completed and actually, no contact was possible given the lack of mail, phone, and internet services.

Jonas had no problem with the lack of human contact in the agreement. There was no significant other currently present in his life and his parents were killed in an automobile accident the year he started graduate school. He readily signed the contract containing the required stipulations and within three days, he, Mo, and Al were on a charted jet to Quebec. From there they were helicoptered to the lab located north of Yellow Knife in the Northwest territories.

Jonas was totally pleased with both the laboratory and its staff. He found the accommodations very satisfactory, if not luxurious and as assistants, Mo and Al proved competent and somewhat aloof. The next step, the primary task ahead, was to establish a research strategy.

Jonas felt strongly that the key to a human life extension procedure lay in the telomeres—the base pairs that formed at the ends of chromosomes. It was widely known that as cells divided, the telomeres were shortened in length with each division. When they reached a certain reduced size, the cell stopped dividing and died, thus contributing to the aging and eventual death of a person.

The logical approach, it would seem, would be to block telomere shortening during cell division. However, a fine line must be observed in this regard since the total termination of telomere reduction would result in an "immortal cell" – the dreaded cancer cell that reproduces uncontrollably. The trick then would be to retard the process, but not eliminate it. His plan, he decided, would be simple. Rather than try to lengthen the telomeres as other researchers had, he would attempt to reduce the amount of shortening associated with each cell division, thus allowing more cell divisions before the terminal length was reached.

For the past eight months, Jonas had been culturing human cells in petri dishes, exposing them to different kinds of telomere protein combinations and checking for the desired reaction. Until on that same cold day in the lab, he finally achieved a positive result.

Jonas couldn't believe it!

He checked with the Electron microscope multiple times and there it was, staring him in the face.

Success!

He hurriedly called Mo to the laboratory and showed him. Mo was ecstatic! They quickly stored Jonas' procedures, data, and results on a flash drive, and Mo arranged helicopter transport to the Quebec airport so that he could take the information for independent verification and ultimately, present it to the Sheik.

After Mo left, Jonas had nothing to do but reflect on possible outcomes. If the results were not able to be verified, he'd be back to the old grind, but if they could…

Jonas entered into a self-induced trance.

He pictured the $2,000,000 addition to his bank account. He envisioned, after the one year wait of course, publishing and being pursued by pharmaceutical companies desirous of his patented procedures. He even saw a possible Nobel prize in his future. Well, nothing to do but wait.

Two weeks later, Al told Jonas that Mo had returned and wished to see them both at once in the lab. When they got to the lab, Mo motioned Jonas to a chair and as he sat down, Mo spoke.

"I have good news. Your process has been successfully verified. The telomeres are shortening at 60% of the normal rate. Based on the statistics, the average human life span will be increased by fifty to sixty years. Congratulations on an excellent job."

Jonas realized at one the implications of these statements. He would become a wealthy and well-known man.

"However," Mo continued, "there is some bad news as well."

"What's the bad news?"

"This!" answered Mo as he pinned Jonas' arms to the chair while Al injected a clear liquid into his vein.

Jonas bolted out of the chair and shouted, "What's going on?"

"Sit down. Sit down," Mo said soothingly. "I will explain everything to you. My name is Mohammed Halie and my associate is Aljatra Kobic. We do not represent the Sheik. We are operatives of Al-Qaeda, the new Al-Qaeda. Since the death of our martyred Osama, we have recognized the futility of violent attacks on Americans. They have proven ineffective and retribution always follows. So, we have decided that instead of killing your people, we will make them live longer.

"Your telomerase protein will be introduced into the U.S. water supply and all bottled water sold in America will also contain it. As the percentage of aging people increase, it will put stress on your Medicare, Medicaid, and Social Security programs. The politicians will not cut these so called "entitlements" for fear of voter reprisals. Thus, the funding for these programs will increase at an exponential rate, leaving much less money for other purposes. Eventually, production will be affected, military spending dramatically cut, and overall GDP will plummet. We will have brought America to its economic knees.

"However, life insurance companies will prosper under this scenario and we are currently purchasing such U.S. companies through shell corporations in the

Cayman Islands. Their profits will help us finance our operations."

"I'm feeling faint," interrupted Jonas. "What did you give me?"

"Ah, yes, the injection," Mo replied. "Well, you see, we couldn't let you warn anyone of our plan. After all, it will take several decades to come to fruition. Don't worry, your death will be painless. It's the least we could do, considering your contribution to our cause."

"Your cause will not succeed," Jonas mumbled. "With an extra fifty or sixty years to innovate, our creative American minds will improve productivity and technology to keep our economy on track."

"We considered that possibility." Mo smiled. "So, we took the liberty of attaching your telomerase protein to a molecule that will not pass through the blood-brain barrier. Thus, although the body will enjoy the beneficial effects, the brain will not.

Jonas, in thirty years, the United States of America will have a population whose majority will be suffering from Alzheimer's, dementia, or senility. We will have conquered the Great Satan, not from without, but from within."

Jonas could no longer think clearly and as he drifted slowly down into eternal sleep, he barely heard the sound of Mo and Al chanting over and over again.

"Allahu Akbar. God is Great."

CHAPTER FIVE

The Darwinian Paradox

During the early hours of a morning in 39, 284 B.C., a hunter left the cave shelter to search for small game after first copulating with a half-awake bleeding baby carrier. This was as it should be since the Neanderthal society of the period had not yet adopted a pair-bonding ritual, thus rendering any fertile female in the clan subject to such mating activity. The joining, as with countless others, since the beginning of the species, produced a common and highly predictable result—the birth of a child.

The members of the clan accepted this event as natural and entirely unremarkable. Little did they realize that with this birth, nature was giving the human race a chance to advance light-years ahead on the evolutionary path.

The child, a boy, was born with a mutant gene on chromosome 14. This particular gene was a master gene and its modification caused several genetic instructions normally appearing in Neanderthal's to reverse. The limbic area of the brain was reconfigured when the gene expressing aggressive behavior and violence was switched off. Another gene, further down the chromosomes, was turned on—fostering an almost God-like attunement with nature. A final long dormant gene was activated. Inherited millions of years ago from a creature not unlike an electric eel, it permitted the pineal gland to store electromagnetic energy obtained from the environment, and subsequently discharge it, not in the form of an electric shock, but rather in an energizing, healthful power similar to that radiated by Reiki practitioners, although amplified by a factor of 10,000.

As the child grew to maturity, he exhibited a remarkable empathy for all living things, and conversely, all living things seemed to benefit from his touch. The cultivation and collection of the various plants and vegetables eaten by the clan was not considered to be an appropriate activity for males. However, when he was involved in the planting, the harvest always proved abundant, and his very act of handling them resulted in produce that was more flavorful and nutritious.

Animals, too, were not immune to his spell. He was able to coax the wild wolf-like creatures that prowled in packs into interacting peaceably with human beings to the extent that they aided in the pursuit of game and the detection of danger.

The greatest benefit, though, was reserved for the members of the clan themselves. Through simple tactile contact, he was able to alleviate pain, heal traumatic injuries such as broken bones and generally improve an individual's well-being. Systemic problems also responded to his powers, and age-related diseases were also helped, although not common due to the Neanderthal's relatively short life span.

The clan elders, while recognizing his unusual abilities, did not overly value them. Since he would not and did not hunt, he was termed "useless", renamed "the Odd One," and relegated to a low status position in the clan's hierarchy. In addition, he was denied access to females for procreation purposes and was required to search the surrounding area for wild and unusual plants that could contribute to the clan's diet.

On one of these trips, he was intercepted by a Cro-Magnon hunting party and forcibly taken to their camp. The Cro-Magnon were somewhat more advanced than their Neanderthal brethren, but were highly superstitious. As with many cultures, they feared what they could not understand, and when the "Odd one" demonstrated his gifts, they branded him an evil spirit and rewarded him with a flint-tipped spear thrust to the heart.

Cautiously, they observed the "Odd One" until body-stiffening, the ultimate sign of death, occurred. They then unceremoniously dragged his corpse outside the camp and abandoned it to the wild beasts. However, the death of an organism does not demand the immediate death of its constituent cells. Thus, the pineal gland continued to store its energy until with all molecular processes shutting down, it released the unmodified charge directly into his body—consuming it in a blinking flash of radiation.

Modern anthropologists would consider the death of the "Odd One" a fate accompli based on the assumption of the survival of the fittest. However, the unfortunate demise was overshadowed by the fact that his unique genetic makeup did not enter into the human gene pool, and thus his special abilities, which would prove crucial to humanity's development were not transmitted to posterity. This would have serious ramifications for man's future well-being.

Nature, though thwarted, was undaunted. Roughly 40,000 years later in a backwater province of the Roman Empire, the identical genetic mutation appeared in a Jewish carpenter's son. Although his powers were appreciated by a small group of followers, he was misunderstood, feared, ridiculed, and hated by those in charge. Like the "Odd One" before him, he did not reproduce before he was prematurely terminated as a criminal. Again, nature was frustrated in her desire to beneficially modify the human genome, but probability would predict that another attempt would eventually be forthcoming.

However, the opportunity for such a change was not to manifest itself. A mere 2300 years after the birth of the carpenter's son, mankind, armed with an awesome technology and under the guise of justifiable war, managed to eradicate itself and every other living thing from the face of the earth—assumedly to the chagrin of a long-departed Darwin. The charred and radioactive planet, bereft of life, continued in its orbit—a mute testimonial to the stupidity of man—until after countless eons, an ever-expanding and reddening sun finally engulfed the ball of rock that humans once called home.

CHAPTER SIX

The Documentary

Peter Fincher was unfazed. The major networks were not enthused with his idea. So, what! He could pitch it to the smaller independent media companies—preferably one that had unsheltered profits and could absorb a tax write-off if necessary. After all, a television program presenting information, eye witness interviews, evidence, and possible capture of a Yeti, Bigfoot, Abdominal snowman, Sasquatch or any of the other myriad names applied to an elusive hairy giant ape-like creature, should certainly create enough excitement to boost Neilson ratings for a willing partner. Public presentations on Anacondas, Great White sharks, poisonous snakes and all manner of all other animals have graced the video menus of National

Geographic, Animal Planet and the various science channels for years. Viewer response as a whole, has proven to be quite good for this type of fare. However, the most riveting shows in Peter's opinion (and the easiest to approve) were programs where something was sought. The search for the Arc of the Covenant, the search for Noah's Ark, the search for the Loch Ness Monster, the search of Captain Kidd's treasure—none of these ever found what they were searching for. Yet the very act of looking captured audiences' attention. It was sort of like televised wrestling—all show and very little substance.

Although the Yeti sightings (under different names of course) have been reported all around the world. Peter felt that the ideal location for the expedition would be the Himalayan region of Tibet and Nepal in South Asia. The actual name "Yeti" was given to the creature by the people indigenous to this area and visual records of its appearance were dated as early as the 1700s. However, there were unique advantages in choosing this site as well. The place is inherently mysterious and isolated. Rumors of strange happenings emanated from the inhabitants there and the Khumjung monastery in the same general vicinity harbored a hairy rug-like object that purported to be a genuine Yeti scalp. The language is spoken in numerous regional dialects which generally can't be understood by speakers of the different oral Tibetan forms much less any outsiders.

Thus, he would need translators to interview eye witnesses living in the surrounding territory. These translators, given the right motivation and a little of the local currency, could interpret the stories and recollections somewhat more dramatically than might otherwise be the case. A bit of sensationalism here and there can stimulate and maintain viewer interest. Terrain would also come into play. The Himalayan mountains are more or less covered with snow throughout the year.

While Peter would want to schedule the trip so that the most favorable weather conditions would be experienced, snow-covered ground would be his most likely prospect. This held two great advantages: first, snow tracks are by and large indistinct unless they are very recently formed. Snow melts, wind changes flake position and more snow eventually falls, all distorting the original shape of the track. Second, the entire crew would be tracking up the area performing the tasks necessary to mount the expedition. It would be a simple matter for him to walk out of the sight of the camp, create some questionable oversize tracks, and then shout to the world the discovery of old Yeti footprints.

As P.T. Barnum said, "There's a sucker born every minute."

Well, thought Peter, *that's entertainment!*

Of course, none of these musing could be expressed to the production company or its sponsors, but what they don't know won't hurt them. *Who knows,* he pondered. *If I sell them on this location and get enough extra footage, I might be able to put together a sequel— "The Search for Shangri-La."*

Five weeks later the deed was done. Peter convinced a small production company to finance the project. While the funding was less than the amount he originally sought, Peter was of the opinion that a gift horse should not be examined too closely. After all, by having the production crew double up on some of the duties, he could still emerge with a tidy profit.

So, with passports and visas in hand, he and his technicians flew to New Delhi, motored to Nepal, and after obtaining the necessary permits and permissions (facilitated by the appropriate bribes) a base camp was finally set up 8000 feet above sea level on the Tibetan side of the Himalayan mountains. Their base consisted of three tents; the first was Peter's private accommodations, the second for the rest of the crew, and the third housed the small portable kitchen for food preparation. Peter had decided to reconnoiter for the first couple of days, so other than his solitary secret jaunt to deposit imitation Yeti fecal droppings which he could pretend to discover later, no one ventured more than 2,000 yards from the camp.

****

The Yeti observed the humans from a higher and distant hidden vantage point. He had come down from his cave high on the mountain to explore the strange odors emanating from the lower level. He viewed the creatures below with a primitive sense of distrust and alarm. The little clan he cohabitated with looked to him, the alpha male, for survival and protection. Instinctually, he continued his observations, identified the alpha male in the group and bided his time.

****

Having finished his survey of the surrounding topography, Peter ordered the initiation of the Yeti search for the next morning. The crew spent the rest of the day preparing and with back packs checked and film in the cameras, they settled in for a welcomed night's rest. However, an evening storm brought in the high winds with snow and the ensuing gale howling around the camp did little to promote rejuvenating sleep. When the men groggily awoke at dawn, they were met with a terrible realization—Peter was gone. His tent was in tatters and his personal items, including his two-way pocket radio, were strewn all over the ground. A search party was formed and rallied forth, but many tracks that had existed had been covered by the effects of the storm A helicopter was called in to comb the area but after two days with no results, the effort was suspended. The crew packed up the equipment and returned home and the production company wrote off the expense against a highly successful sitcom that they had produced.

Fifty years later, two villagers climbed the mountain hunting a Himalayan brown bear that had been decimating their herd of goats. Peering up the side of a cliff, they spotted a cave opening once shielded by ice, but now with the effects of Global Warming, it was revealed to the naked eye. Arriving at the entrance they, entered to find the shelter abandoned. Shrugging their shoulders, the hunters left to pursue the bear. Had they bothered to tread further into the cave, they would have noticed the crude drawings chiseled into the cave wall where decades ago, a Yeti had recorded for posterity the tracking, capture, and eventual demise of a creature that was referred to as the "hairless one."

CHAPTER SEVEN

The Testament
of Lazarus

It was a dreary nondescript morning in November when Jackson Gros, the curator of the Biblical manuscripts at the Vatican, received a mysterious phone call. The man was brief.

"Can't talk, must meet; your office two o'clock this afternoon."

The caller disconnected leaving Jackson in a quandary. He had previously made luncheon plans for today. Having no means of contacting the caller, he reluctantly rescheduled lunch for the next day and devoted the remainder of the morning to the contemplation and anticipation of this unusual meeting.

Precisely at two o'clock, a brief knock was heard followed by the speedy opening of his office door. In rushed a man, obviously agitated, who introduced himself as Larry Patterson, then promptly deposited himself in the chair nearest Jackson's desk.

"I am being watched," he said.

Jackson turned toward the man and asked him for an explanation. The man told him that he was a Historical novelist and was given access to the Vatican secret library to obtain information for a biography of Pope Alexander the VI.

While examining the pope's papers, he found a Latin translation of an older Greek text hidden among the documents. Being fluent in Latin, he translated the script into English and was astounded to realize that the document was attributed to Lazarus.

Jackson was in shock. "Is it another rendition of Jesus' life—another gospel?"

"No, No!" Larry replied. "It begins after Lazarus was raised from the dead." Larry went on to explain that several days after coming out of the tomb, Lazarus was bothered by strange memories and he went promptly to Jesus because he was disturbed by them.

Jesus calmed Lazarus and asked him to describe what he remembered. Lazarus said that in one memory he was a woman. She lived in a cave with others of her kind and dressed in animal skins because it was very cold. Her mate hunted strange animals using a spear.

When he wasn't hunting, he drew pictures of the animals on the cave walls. This dream-like memory ended when she died giving birth.

Another memory that surfaced for him appeared to be of a different age from the first. He was a man this time. He had some kind of pack strapped to his back and was inside a machine that allowed him to fly through the air like a bird. Other machines were flying around in the air too. Inside the machine were levers and knobs that could be pressed to shoot small bits of metal to hit the other flying machines. His machine had a flame appear on it and it plummeted from the sky with him inside.

Jesus told Lazarus not to be troubled. This was simply a consequence of his being raised from the dead. Jesus reminded Lazarus of the precept that, unless a person is born again, he cannot enter into the kingdom of heaven.

Lazarus was puzzled. "I am familiar with that teaching, but isn't that why you and John the Baptist baptized the followers?"

Jesus looked kindly at Lazarus as a parent would to a child. "I speak in parables to the masses so that they can grasp the essence of my meaning as they are not ready to comprehend the ultimate truth. However, I will initiate you into the higher plane of knowledge."

Jesus then reminded Lazarus of his preaching about how difficult and impossible it was for man to achieve justification in order to merit heaven. However, as Jesus pointed out, with God all things are possible. He gives you many opportunities through multiple lives to correct mistakes, grow in wisdom, and perfect yourself so that eventually all will be candidates for heavenly reward. This secret is not to be revealed to all because of the possibility of abuse. If everyone knows they can achieve salvation through other lives, it may lead to wantonness and misbehavior in this one with the knowledge that they can make it up in the other.

"Who else is aware of this teaching?" Lazarus asked.

Jesus replied, "Other than you, only the Baptist, my mother, and Mary Magdalen have knowledge of this." Jesus paused thoughtfully, then added, "Judas Iscariot will be told at the proper time in light of the task which he has been ordained to perform."

"And Peter?" Lazarus inquired.

"After I am gone, the Holy Spirit will come and infuse this knowledge into the remaining apostles so that they can endure the hardships and tribulations of preaching the gospel with the confidence of knowing they will be justly rewarded."

Larry stated, "Lazarus seemed satisfied with that response and thanked Jesus for sharing this knowledge, and that's where the text ends."

Jackson was amazed at the tale revealed by Larry. "This find is historic! This means just as bread and wine are symbols of the Christ's death and sacrifice for us, water baptism represents the rebirth of life with the amniotic fluid." Jackson leaned toward Larry. "You say you found this text hidden in the papers of Pope Alexander VI?"

"Yes, it's still there. There was no way I could remove it. Security is too tight."

"Stands to reason," Jackson muttered. "This was the pope who had mistresses, many children, and was known for political intrigues. He had to be aware of this teaching."

Suddenly the office door opened and in stepped a monsignor holding a silenced Glock pistol in his hand.

"Ah, Mr. Gros, Mr. Patterson," he said. "How unfortunate that you have obtained this information. Obviously, the church cannot allow this teaching of multiple lives and eventual salvation for all to be made public. It would eliminate our ability to control our congregation."

Two silenced shots were fired and as blood slowly dripped onto the hardwood floor, Jackson and Larry were being prepared for their next lives.

CHAPTER EIGHT

'Til Death Do Us Part

I won't hear of it, Joan. You've only been married three years. Is he cheating on you?"

"No, daddy," Joan answered.

"Then you and Alfred make up and get some counseling!" her father yelled and hung up the phone on her.

That went well, thought Joan sarcastically as she returned her phone to its cradle. No question she resented her dad's intrusion into her personal life, but Howard Baker, Chairman and CEO of Baker Enterprises was one of the most successful businessmen in the state of Virginia, and more importantly, he set up and controlled the reversable trust that paid his daughter's $15,000 a month income, so Daddy's opinions were not to be ignored. Anyway, she was the one push-ing for the divorce.

Alfred Lancaster, her husband, had entered into marriage with few expectations and therefore was not overly disappointed with the results. Basically, his pas-sion was politics. After obtaining a Political Science degree, struggling through law school, and setting up a marginally successful legal practice, he set his sights on public service. Marriage lent an air of stability to that venture, but divorce did not play well, especially among female voters.

Joan thought very little of his political aspirations. He was not handsome and not charismatic, although he could speak extemporaneously with the best of them. His fatal flaw though was his constant obsession with truth and honesty. How in the world could he ex-pect to become an electable politician without relying on B.S. and a "You scratch my back, I'll scratch your back philosophy?"

God! He is so naïve, she thought.

Alfred had also expressed an interest in starting a family, but Joan was quick to point out that children were not high on her list of priorities, and when she dis-covered that Negro blood had entered the Lancaster family tree eight or nine generations back, she abso-lutely put her foot down.

"I will not give birth to a zebra," she declared, although the likelihood of any African-American traits appearing in a child sired by Alfred were remote at best.

Neither Joan nor Alfred had a strong sex drive so that disparity, common to many marriages, was not evident here. Joan's dissatisfaction stemmed from a perceived need for more attention. Raised by a wealthy father and a doting mother, the former debutante majored in drama in college and the limelight of the stage suited her perfectly. Even though she did not pursue an acting career after graduation, she maintained a strong dramatic interest and served on the board of the local repertory theatre. She tried to attend plays with Alfred, but he insisted that he suffered a headache every time he went, and his refusal to share with her something she so enjoyed led to outright feeling of alienation. She turned play attendance to a solitary activity and sought solace in her obsession with the romance and history of the Old South.

Being from Virginia, she was enamored with Robert E. Lee, read many of his biographies, and through him became acquainted with the chivalrous Southern culture of his time. She longed to have been romanced during that period and went so far as to become a quazi-expert on antebellum plantation era. However, it was no panacea and she remained disillusioned with matrimony.

Alfred readily agreed to the counseling plan. He really didn't want a divorce in the first place, and he was also well aware that her trust fund provided the majority of their incomes. An appointment with a marriage counselor was thus duly made and kept. After the first session the counselor sensed Joan's deep animosity and quickly recommended a trial separation so both Joan and Alfred could work on their individual issues. Joan immediately claimed the house and Alfred was remined of that old saying "25% of men kiss their wife goodbye when they leave their house, but 99% of men kiss their house goodbye when they leave their wife."

It must apply to separations too, he thought as he proceeded to rent and occupy a small apartment. Joan, for her part, reveled in her newly-found freedom. She applied for and received a permit to carry a concealed weapon and proudly displayed to the counselor a small handgun in her purse as a symbol of her independence.

Having had several additional meetings with Alfred and Joan, the counselor, realizing more drastic steps were required, arranged appointments for both of them with licensed medical hypnotists. Doctor Jack Collins for Alfred and Doctor Michael Parker for Joan. They would be given individual regression analysis and the two doctors would then compare notes and results to formulate a plan of action.

Alfred had the first appointment and at its conclusion, Dr. Collins replayed the taped session and then contacted Dr. Parker. Collins told Parker that he regressed Alfred to a past life where he appeared to be some kind of labor organizer and activist. He had made speeches about maintaining a union and had encouraged violent confrontations to achieve that goal. He felt responsible for those killed and injured in these confrontations and the guilt he carried certainly shaped his personality.

Parker thanked Collins for the info and hoped that future regressions would be more enlightening.

Two days later, it was Joan's turn. Her fragmented regression indicated a past life as a man, probably a Roman soldier. There was a fall in which his leg was injured. This was accompanied by some Latin phrase most likely a vernacular obscenity triggered by the pain. Then there was a series of horseback rides alternating with periods of hiding, an ineffectual stop for medical care, a futile attempt to seek refuge in a wooden structure. All in all, neither doctor considered the information helpful.

Alfred had mentioned to Dr. Collins the strange occurrence of headaches associated with play attendance. And, after consulting with Dr. Parker, they recommended that he attend a play with someone other than his wife.

Accordingly, Alfred purchased two tickets for a repertory theatre production on the 24th of the month, and asked a co-worker to accompany him. Unfortunately, he put the transaction on a credit card and when the bill came to the house, Joan exploded.

That bastard, she thought. *He won't take me but he'll take someone else.*

Alfred's next regression appointment was on the morning of the 24th and as soon as it was completed, Dr. Collins was on the phone with Dr. Parker.

"Michael," he said. "You are not going to believe this. He wasn't a labor organizer. He was trying to preserve the Union of the States. The guilt he felt was for war casualties. When I regressed him further, I heard his speech at Gettysburg. Alfred Lancaster was Abraham Lincoln!"

Dr. Parker was silent for almost a minute then he replied, "I'll call you back."

Three hours later, Dr. Collins got the return call.

"Jack," Dr. Michael Parker said, "we have a serious problem on our hands. Joan knows about Alfred's theatre plans this evening and she's ticked off. Also, I replayed her regression tapes the phrase that I thought was profanity is actually 'Sic seimper tyrannis'—Thus always to tyrants. It is the same phrase that Lincoln's assassin uttered when he jumped from the balcony to the stage at Ford's theatre. To top it off, the marriage counselor says she carrying a derringer in her handbag. I think Joan, in her past life, was John Wilkes Booth!"

"Oh my God! Jack exclaimed. "No wonder they weren't compatible. How are we going to handle this?"

"I don't know," Michael Parker replied. "But whatever you do, don't let Alfred attend that play tonight!"

CHAPTER NINE

Who Dares Call
It Treason

I don't believe it," exclaimed George, "not Benny!"

"Sir, the evidence is irrefutable," replied the mayor.

Washington sat back in his chair, stunned. How could his best general have suddenly become a British collaborator? It just didn't make sense, considering his knowledge of Benedict's background. When the war broke out, the Connecticut-born Arnold was operating a fleet of merchant ships. He immediately joined the army and proceeded to distinguish himself by demonstrating intelligence and bravery in his personal conduct. He played a key role in the capture of Fort

Ticonderoga, the Battle if Ridgefield—after which he received a promotion to Major General—and the Battle of Saratoga.

It was in this last series of battles that he incurred leg injuries which required his recuperation for a period of time. Despite his stellar performance in the field, congress pointedly ignored his achievements and promoted other less deserving officers to more responsible commands, and to Arnold's mortification, his accomplishments were attributed to those officers as well.

Generally unpopular in the military and political circles, Arnold's adversaries brought corruption and maleficence charges against him. Even though he was eventually acquitted, they continued to investigate his accounts despite the fact that he spent much of his own money to support the war.

He had communicated with Washington over this sad state of affairs, but George, having his own issues with the congress, was unable to assist him. Although Benedict was unhappy with his situation and noting that the political infighting in congress was causing depreciation of the currency, disaffection of the army and impeding the war effort, he resolutely backed the colonists' struggle for freedom.

The persecution continued when Benedict was appointed Commandant of Philadelphia. He was summarily brought up for two counts of profiteering from the war. Though he was convicted, Arnold thought the charges unfounded and politically motivated. Washington, for his part, was especially chagrined and referred to the charges against benedict as "peculiarly reprehensible."

His first wife, Margaret Mansfield, bore him three sons before dying in 1775. Having been deeply involved with his army duties, Benedict remained a widower until his Philadelphia assignment at which point, he met and married, Peggy Shippen, the 19-year-old daughter of a wealthy British sympathizer. The marriage raised a number of eyebrows in the colonies, not only for their considerable age difference but more importantly for the diametrically opposed positions each represented.

Arnold saw himself as a Freedom fighter. Her family saw him as a revolutionary. Even his fellow generals commented on this union and questioned his loyalty based on his present association with Tories.

Washington, however, had no qualms about Arnold's intentions and demonstrated his confidence by promoting him to the position of Commander at the fort in West Point, New York—a key position. The fort overlooked the New York harbor and controlling it was essential to maintaining a supply route for the army. Should its defensive protection be lost, it could cost the colonies the war.

Arnold gladly accepted the post and moved there with his new wife in the latter part of 1779. Upon his arrival, he was confronted with an almost untenable situation. The fort was in deplorable condition. Supplies and munitions were almost non-existent, and morale among the troops was pitiful. Arnold wrote to Washington immediately requesting money and supplies so that he could shore up this vital structure against attack and to insure its ability to defend the harbor.

Washington forwarded Arnold's request as well as supplications of his own to congress, but political intrigue and lack of appreciation for military strategy derailed the expected aid. Arnold consulted again with Washington to no avail and then reluctantly decided on a course of action. He secretly contacted John Andre, a former suitor of his spouse and a major in the British army who was recently named Chief of English spies.

Arnold offered Andre copies of the plans and layout of the West Point fort in exchange for some money and a general's rank in the army of Great Britain. Andre quickly passed the offer along to Sir Henry Clinton the Commander of the British forces. Clinton, recognizing the importance of the information, readily acceded to Benedict's demands.

Arnold drew up the plans, gave them to his wife and she incorporated them in a letter which she subsequently sent to Andre. He, in turn, was to smuggle the information to General Clinton. However, the

Americans intercepted Andre along the route, confiscated the papers and sent them both straight to Washington.

George after examining the incriminating document outlying the make-up and substandard conditions at the fort and determining them to be written in Benedict's hand, reluctantly signed an order for his arrest. Arnold already aware of Andre's capture, was at that moment, fleeing down the Hudson river in a British warship.

From this vantage point, he composed a final letter to Washington outlining the reasons for the plot. In it he explained that its purpose was to outrage and infuriate the colonists by exposing the critical nature and congressional neglect of the fort. He also pointed out that it was his anonymous tip that ultimately prevented Andre from successfully reaching Clinton. Finally, he begged Washington to provide safe passage for his wife back to her family in Philadelphia, a request that George quickly granted. He ended the communication with the statement that "love for my country actuates my present conduct, however it may appear inconsistent to the world, who very seldom judges right of any man's action."

After the successful conclusion of the war, Washington wrote Arnold who was now residing in London. He told Benedict that the circumstances surrounding his treachery produced the desired effect and congress appropriated funds not only for the fort but sufficient to finance the rest of the conflict as well. He praised Arnold and stated that the sacrifice of his reputation incurred because of his apparent betrayal was a uniquely patriotic act and for his part in the birthing of a new nation, he should be recognized as one of its fathers.

However, Washington emphasized that he would not be able to pursue Benedict's public vindication. Being pressured from all quarters to accept the presidency of the newly-formed republic, Washington agreed, not to satisfy political ambition, but to ensure that the reins of government were not passed to someone self-serving or incompetent, and he was intent on devoting his efforts solely to that daunting task. Washington ended his correspondence with a fond and heartfelt farewell.

Benedict reread the letter several times, then put it down. Slowly, a feeling of quiet contentment filled his spirit for now he knew that although he was branded a traitor by his former country, he was considered a hero by its first president.

CHAPTER TEN

Who's Your Daddy?

250,000 B.C.

The robot awoke from its programmed slumber. After eons and eons of travel originating from the other side of the galaxy, the space craft's sensors had detected a planet in close proximity which would provide a suitable habitat for the cosmic seed being transported. The Old Ones, an ancient race of human beings, when faced with total annihilation from an impending Gamma ray burst, flooded the surrounding Galactic neighborhood with such ships in the hope that their efforts would prevent the extinction of the human organism.

The robot was completely dispassionate. It cared not for the noble endeavors of its creators. It only responded to the logical programs residing in its memory banks. Fate and providence held no computational value so the robot would not and could not appreciate the happy coincidence that on the newly discovered planet, a 65-million-year old planetary collision with an asteroid removed animal life that was incompatible with their repopulation goals and created an ideal environment for the achievement of the robot's task. The robot simply commenced work.

First, it surveyed the planet considering the human requirements of available water, food, temperate climate, non-threatening animal life, and proceeded to pilot the craft to that location. After landing, the robot accessed its programming directives and began to analyze the planet's crust in order to obtain, prepare, and synthesize the chemicals and materials necessary to form the two human bodies required for the preservation of the species.

Due to the long and elaborate child rearing necessitated for human development, the two human beings produced were to be adults. It searched through its biological files for the human male recipe, identifying the appropriate genome, setting the matrix, and inserting the proper genome with the separate X and Y chromosomes into the coalescing human form. As the bones, ligaments, tendons, organs, and muscle tissue developed, the dendrites and neurons in the brain simultaneously formed enumerable synapses and the billon connections necessary to reproduce the sapiens capacity for intelligence.

When the male body was complete, the same process was employed for the female, substituting an additional X chromosome in place of the masculine Y. However, there was another required procedure. It was impossible, of course, to create identical twins because of the sex difference. None the less, it had been deemed desirable to have the compatibility of the two bodies as biologically close as possible. Thus, the robot employed the added step of removing a bone from the male, injecting the bone and the accompanying bone marrow into the female, insuring that the two individuals would share the same blood types and other biochemical characteristics.

The last step was the programming of the male and female brains with the information required to insure the perpetuation, reproduction, and ultimate survival of the species. This included environmental details involving types of animals and plants, techniques on cultivating both for food, instructional knowledge specific to both sexes (aggressive and protective tendencies in the male, nurturing and intuitive tendencies in the female) and the instillation in both brains of a set of social norms and mores from which an established pattern of behavior based on a concept of right and wrong could emerge. The culmination of this brain manipulation was the electrical stimulation of the penial gland which sent life coursing through the bodies of the newly created human beings.

Its primary function fulfilled, the robot reentered the space craft and flew out into space, a cosmic Johnny Appleseed, searching for its next opportunity to spread humanity throughout the galaxy.

****

2032 A.D.

Tom Gasper was sitting in his office at the University of Maryland when he received a phone call from an old college friend, an anthropologist excavating in the Middle East.

"Mike! How are you? Long-time no-hear."

Mike cantor could scarcely contain his excitement. "Tom, you're not going to believe what I've discovered. We were digging near the Tigris-Euphrates river valley and uncovered the mummified bodies of a man and a woman."

"Hold on, Mike," Tom said. "Mummified remains in the Middle East aren't that remarkable."

"But Tom," Mike exclaimed. "They've been carbon-dated. The bodied are 248,000 years old plus or minus 20,000 years.

"Mike," Tom replied. "I'm a Biblical archeologist not an anthropologist. Are you sure they're not hominids?"

"Absolutely not," Tom stated. "They're definitely Homo Sapiens. Anyway, I'm calling about another question. Isn't the area where I'm working the general vicinity where the Garden of Eden supposedly existed?"

Tom sighed. "Yes, Mike. Years ago it was considered to be in that region, but in this day and age, Eden is thought of as a mythical location in a non-factual bible story.

"Well, Tom," Mike countered. "Here's a fact for you. Neither of the bodies has an umbilicus."

"What does that mean?" Tom demanded.

"They don't have belly-buttons," Mike stated triumphantly. "And guess what? The man is missing a rib!"

ACKNOWLEDGEMENTS

I would like to thank my daughter, Laurie Bolanos, for her invaluable contribution without whose help this book would never have been published.

I would also like to thank my family for their encouragement and support.

I would like to recognize Christy Nichols for formatting services and Christine Hoover for proofreading.

I would to thank my grandson, Alex Bolanos, for his thoughtful comments.

And lastly, I'd like to thank you, the reader, for perusing this collection of stories and I hope you found it entertaining.

ABOUT THE AUTHOR

Earl is a retired math teacher and accountant, as well as an accomplished musician and composer who was inducted into the Louisiana Music Hall of Fame. His compositions and playing can be heard on YouTube music and CDbaby.com under the artist name, Barry Lacour. When he isn't playing saxophone, he enjoys reading, writing, working out, spending time with his cats, and cruising with his wife of 50-plus years.

www.ingramcontent.com/pod-product-compliance
Lightning Source LLC
Chambersburg PA
CBHW020316150626
46552CB00022B/2902